...ope you enjoy reading
and remember :
Dont kill mum ! :)

Mondays

Love from your
big bro,
#Kobayaashi

Kobayaashi

Mondays

Jai Kobayaashi Gomer

Kobayaashi

First Edition.
First Printing 2021.

Published by Kobayaashi Studios.
www.kobayaashi.co.uk
All enquiries : info@kobayaashi.co.uk

Printed in the United Kingdom.

The '*upturned K*' logo is a TradeMark of Kobayaashi Studios.
Cover Design & Artwork by Jai Kobayaashi Gomer.

ISBN : 978-1-8383648-0-9

Dedicated to my beautiful wife, in recognition of her love, support and understanding, without which I would be nothing...

In the beginning, a man lives in misery with his overbearing, nagging mother in a rambling, damp and unpleasant house. The grating sound of her voice disgusts him as much as do the foul odours which emanate from her fat, bloated frame.

One night, unable to bear the suffocating stench of her any more, he kills her, smashing a hammer into the side of her head without warning, and there is joy in his relief as she silently slumps to the floor.

He stands over her prone corpse, breathing softly in the stillness of the room. The only other sound is the ticking of a clock, marking out the seconds of his new-found freedom.

..

He wakes the next morning, remembers that he is free, and smiles.

Later, he watches the world go by beyond the unwashed glass of the living room window as he makes plans to dispose of the body.

He smokes a cigarette as he watches neighbours and strangers passing through the street, making their way from one part of their life to another. From home to work. From friends to family. It angers him to know that he envies them.

He imagines being discovered by them, pictures their faces as they spy undignified death on the worn, stained carpet. He tells himself that they are caged within their lives, while he has freed himself from torment and ridicule and pain. He watches from behind the window, smiling.

That night, he drags the massive bulk of her body through the house, and into the garden. He grunts as he grabs her flesh, straining to force it up and onto a wheelbarrow. It slips and falls. The barrow keeps tipping. He kicks at her body, and curses under his breath. He searches his toolshed for twine, and uses that to lash the body to the barrow, and a spade to the body.

He uses the winter darkness as cover to take her body out to a place where he can dig a shallow grave. He wheels the barrow through the back lanes, free from the glare of tell-tale street lights, stopping on occasion to reposition the load.

He reaches the place, and begins to dig. He grunts and sweats, and curses her once more for being so fat that he needs to dig such a large hole. When it is done, he tips the body into the ground, covers it with earth, and returns home to wash the mud and the blood from his body.

In the morning he wakes, remembers that he is free, and smiles widely as he savours the uninterrupted silence of his morning routine. He sits on the toilet, farting freely, knowing that he won't hear her shout her disgust at him from her room, despite her own filthy emanations. He brushes his teeth, spits, and looks up at himself in the mirror above the sink.

He sees that he is smiling. He thinks that this makes his face appear strange. He has never liked his face, as it made him think of her, but now it is different. When he smiles, he doesn't look like her.

He spends a while trying out different smiles, hoping to find one which fits his face.

Later, he heads downstairs, still smiling.

Then he sees her body, swollen limbs slumped in the carpet's filth, as he had left it the night he killed her.

His shock, fear and confusion catch his breath, and bring him to his knees. His mouth drops open, but no words come out. He shrinks back against the wall in fear, thinking perhaps he had dreamed the day before, while something inside him screams that this is not right.

And then, the world outside begins to happen as it already has done once before. He hears the sounds of the same passing conversations in the street outside. He creeps to the window to peer out through the smeared, stained glass. Watches his neighbours pass by in the same order as the previous day. People, cars, patterns repeat.

Unexpectedly, he vomits. He wipes his face with one trembling hand. He closes his eyes and tries to slow his breathing. He tells himself this is not real. He tells himself this is not real. He tells himself this is not real. He opens his eyes, and the world outside the window screams back into his face.

This is real.

..

He sits crouched in a corner of the room, his mind spinning with the absurdity of the world, while his mother lies on the grubby, pock-marked carpet, mocking him with her presence.

..

Later, he drags her body through the house, heaves it onto a wheelbarrow, and wheels it out under cover of darkness, burying her in a shallow grave in the same spot as before. He returns home, exhausted, and washes the mud and the blood from himself before sinking into bed.

He wakes, remembers, and his heart pounds hard as he makes his way to the room, just to check.

When he sees her body there as before, fear shoots

through his blood like ice, and erupts as vomit.

Later, he hides in the room with the body, watches the world happen through torn curtains, and wonders many things.

He watches the unfolding of the day with amazed eyes. He discovers the wonder of watching an action occur for the second or third time, being able to experience details missed when they first occurred. He wonders for a while whether he might be dead. Or perhaps driven mad at the moment of murder.

Still, he is bound to his actions, and the results of his actions, and that night he makes the same laborious journey with the body-laden barrow, only with less concern than before, angry that he must repeat the process.

He returns, washes, drinks and sleeps.

He wakes, remembers, and heads downstairs, to see the body where it was, where it should never have been.

He rails at the Universe, and at Life, viciously kicking

at the lifeless body taking up space on his carpet.

He sits out on his front step for a smoke. His first visibly different act.

The world turns. He watches.

A neighbour, who on other days had narrowly avoided colliding with a car, offers a greeting to the man and, in doing so, diverts their attention, gets hit by the car, and dies broken in the street. A passing pedestrian comes to help, is struck in turn by a different car, and the sound of tyres screeching and bones cracking fills the morning air.

The man heads back inside, trembling. His nose bleeds. The body is still there, taunting.

That night, he takes the body once more to the spot, but his digging is without heart. In the end, he just dumps the burdensome cadaver, vaguely covering it with earth and leaves. He returns home, not bothering to wash, he just drinks, and sleeps.

He wakes, remembers. Looks out at the world from his bedroom window, and sees it is all the same.

He heads down to the body. Watches it for a while. Heads to the kitchen and makes a coffee.

He takes his coffee to the front step, with a cigarette.

The world turns. He watches.

Then, there is a woman. Watching him.

She is a new thing.

..

After watching each other for the longest time, she approaches, and sits next to him.

She shares a cigarette with him.

They sit in silence. He tries to form the words, to ask whether she is suffering as he is.

Without warning, she turns and begins to punch him, viciously, repeatedly. He tries to fend her off, but she is crazed. Then, just as abruptly, she stops attacking him, and leaves, walking off with only the slightest backward glance.

He watches her go, in utter confusion, blood dripping down his face, bruises welling up.

He doesn't follow her.

His neighbour walks by, offers a greeting. There is a screech of breaks, and a thud. And another.

Later, he doesn't wait for night to fall, instead taking the body out in the early evening, knowing that he will be seen.

Some people are shocked at the sight, some take pictures on their phones, others call the police.

He doesn't dig, or even bother to take the wheelbarrow away, merely leaves both at the spot where too many times he has dug a grave.

He seems relieved to see the police.

The cell door slams shut, he lays down on the mattress, closes his eyes, and sleeps.

He wakes.

In his own bed.

And screams.

..

Later that morning, she is there again.

She sits alongside him, sharing a cigarette. He asks her not to hit him again. She apologises. He asks her to watch, and she does so, as his neighbour falls victim once again to his new fate.

He explains to her that originally, the neighbour was not distracted by his presence, and so had avoided the accident, and lived. He explains that he holds no animosity to his neighbour, but that he has since sat on the step on purpose, as some kind of macabre fuck-you to Fate.

She explains that she has lived the same day for so long she has forgotten the others that came before. She has become somewhat unhinged, and prone to outbursts of violence, to which he was witness the previous day.

They continue to sit and smoke, as the horror in the street plays out.

He tells her his name is Scully. She tells him her name is Camille.

He tells her he has killed his mother.

..

They both head indoors to see the body, still where it was left that first morning.

When asked, he tells her that he's buried the body a number of times before, but has rather given up on the idea. If the world were to reset, he would be happy to accept the consequences of his actions. In the meantime, however, it would still be nice to have it out of the room.

She helps him to move the body into a spare room.

They enjoy an afternoon of television, pizza and alcohol.

And loud sex.

Afterwards, she asks him what he would like to do. He has no idea.

She tells him of some of her exploits. Sex with random strangers, sometimes taking them home, sometimes fucking in public, in the most crowded of spaces. Mindless acts of violence. She tells him how she robbed a shop at knifepoint, making the prick of an owner cry.

She tells him how she has tried to kill herself.

She tells him to fuck her again, to get rid of the misery. He does so. She cries.

..

He asks her whether she'd like to go and see a film, and the two of them laugh at the screen, pigging out on popcorn, sweets and coke.

They touch one another, to the disgust of those seated around them.

..

He wakes. She is knocking on his front door.

She asks him whether he has any money.

When he asks why, she tells him she's never been on holiday. She wants to go on holiday.

..

They are on a train. They ride it further and further from home, watching their life pass away behind them. She seems almost content, for the moment.

In the carriage, people are living their lives. Lives filled with yesterdays and tomorrows, not just todays.

He asks her how her journey began. She tells him.

She tells him that her life was empty, painfully so. Relationships were fleeting and abusive. She was caught in a never-ending cycle of misery. Sex and drugs and tears. She hated herself. One night, she drank herself into a stupor, cut her wrists and bled out into a bath. It took a while. She hadn't done a great job. Then she woke up, in her bed, to face the misery again. Her wounds were gone, like it had all been a bad dream, but her pain and self-loathing remained, and did so for the longest time.

And now? He asks her.

She watches the world pass by the window. The faintest of smiles is born.

..

Night has fallen. They sit on the sandy beach, watching the black sea roll in and out under a blacker sky.

He asks her whether she thinks this day will ever end. She tells him she doesn't want it to. They hold hands, fingers interlaced, on the sand.

They are both smiling.

He wakes.

Smiling.

..

That morning, he turns on the radio, moves the body out of the room, cleans the place up, washes dishes and makes breakfast while he waits for her.

Outside, his neighbour passes by, avoiding an accident.

The breakfast is cold, and she's still not there.

He begins to worry.

He opens his door to look out onto the street.

He realises he doesn't know where she lives.

He turns off the radio, leaving the house silent.

After a while, there is a loud thud at his front door. He rushes to it; opens it to find her slumped, bloodied, on his step.

He drags her, semi-conscious, into his kitchen. Keeps her awake, washes the blood from her, asks her what happened.

She slurs words through her bloody mouth.

He panics. Begs her to be okay.

He is scared.

..

She is in the bath. He finds her towels, and a dressing gown to wear. He washes her, gently, cleaning the remaining spots of blood from her face.

Eventually, she speaks.

She woke as she has done for forever, but this time she was still smiling from the moment before she woke. She was eager to see him, and left the house early, to head to his place. On the way, however, she took a detour. She wanted to buy him something special, and there was a shop she knew...

On an unfamiliar street, she encountered a man. She should have been paying more attention. Would have been, if she hadn't been so wrapped up in her own unusual happiness.

He moved towards her as she was about to pass him. He blocked her way. He grabbed her. She struggled, and he began to beat her. It seemed to make no difference to him that people were watching. For their part, they watched on in horror, nobody lifting a finger to help her as the man viciously kicked and punched her, screaming unintelligible hatred into her face.

After a while, she noticed that he was no longer beating her. She looked around as best she could, through blood and tears, but he had gone. Still, nobody came to help. She had dragged herself to Scully's house, and fallen against his door.

He watches as she cries.

Soon afterwards, he leads her to the bed, and lays her down gently. He lays next to her, and holds her. He strokes her hair, and she sleeps.

..

He wakes. Dresses. Pulls two sharp knives from a kitchen drawer, and puts them in his jacket pocket. He waits.

She knocks on his door.

He leaves at a determined pace, she with him.

As if it were written, and could be no other way, they make their way wordlessly to the street, moving as one. It is a little later in the morning, but the man is still there. Still screaming incoherent obscenities. Across the road a police car has pulled up, one officer on the radio, another surveying the street.

Scully hands her a knife.

Without pausing their determined strides, they head straight for the man, each gripping tightly the knife in their hand. His eyes register confusion, and he seems stunned at the immediate ferocity of the two attackers, his mouth open wide in a silent, Munchian scream as the two blades slide in and out of his body.

The street is filled with blood and screams and fear.

..

Later, he sits cuffed to a table in a bleak, depressing interview room at a police station.

A button is pressed. This interview is recorded.

There is no reason, no need, to lie. Only a need to know where to begin.

He begins before the beginning. He tells them that he has killed his mother.

..

He wakes. Remembers.

He curls into a ball, and cries.

..

They are sat at a cafe, talking, while the world turns the same turn it has turned so many times before.

He wonders how many others there are out there. Wonders whether the man who had beaten her had been driven mad by the Day, or had merely been mad.

She's not sure whether this is all the fault of science or religion, but thinks it must be one or the other.

He stands up in the cafe and announces that he is living the same day over and over, and calls for all those doing likewise to show themselves.

He is ignored.

..

Walking along the street, he asks to see where she lives.

She tries to stall, but eventually, reluctantly, agrees.

..

On the way, they pass a scene. Police, a broken body cordoned off with tape, cars, vans and silent blue flashing lights. The aftermath of bloody violence. Bordering the scene, the crowd : eagerly-curious faces, death's horror dispersed across social networks as a souvenir.

..

They reach her place. She seems embarrassed. The place is a mess. Now that she's kind of happy, she wants to keep it clean, but every morning it returns to the same state it was in on that ugly day before all this began.

She hates that she must always wake up here.

He hates that he is powerless to ease her unhappiness.

He says he's sorry for insisting on coming here.

He says, they could always burn it down.

He shops, returning with petrol, firelighters, matches and alcohol.

They put on music, and drink while they dance while they douse the place with fuel.

From the street, they watch as the flames take hold, devouring the building. They hold hands. They stink of petrol. Their clothes are scorched.

A hard-faced man approaches them, asks for a light.

They offer a light, and he accepts with thanks.

He tells them his name is Eric.

He tells them, this didn't happen yesterday.

What didn't happen? They ask.

This building didn't burn down yesterday. Yesterday it was fine. Today is different.

In the street, the building begins to collapse.

..

It's mid-morning. They're sat with Eric, the hard-faced man, in a cafe.

He tells them he's seen them about. His attention gained when things happened which did not happen before. His curiosity piqued when blood began to flow. Then he saw the fire, and found them watching.

They ask him how long he's been in the Day.

He hesitates for a moment, tells them. Twelve years. Give or take a few days.

They absorb this new information with quiet, mid-morning terror.

He tells them that the life he lived before the Day has become as an illusion, the only reality being the Day. The everlasting Day.

They ask him whether he knows why, or how. He tells them he has no idea.

They ask him whether he knows of others. He tells them yes. He invites them to his place. On the way, he'll introduce them to one of the others.

..

In a grim part of town, on a patch of wasteland an abandoned building, open to the elements, alongside a busy pedestrian street. Littered with rubbish and filth. Huddled in a corner, a figure.

Muttering quietly.

They move with stealth, finding a spot where they can see and hear the figure, without being seen in return. Eric tells them. Listen.

The figure mutters a quiet, staccato barrage of nonsense.

Eric then nods towards the street.

Then they see.

Though the figure is blind to the street, wrapped up against the cold with a varied assortment of clothes and an old blanket, the mutterings are an exact telling of every movement in the street, mere moments before they occur.

The tired woman with the ugly child.

The man with the green hair, who drops his keys.

The barking dog.

The man about to light a cigarette.

Soon it will rain.

..

They ask Eric what they had seen. He tells them that he had encountered the man years before. Disturbed him in his prophetic rant.

He tells them that that's what happens when a day lasts forty years.

..

Eric takes them to his place. It's an established mess of beer stains, discarded cigarettes and leftover food. They watch television. Smoke. Drink.

He watches Camille.

He takes a fresh bottle from the fridge. Drinks a little. Then smashes it over Scully's head.

In his semi-conscious state, Scully watches as Camille fights with Eric, struggling, suffering beneath his blows.

When she stops resisting, he rapes her.

Scully watches, helplessly, unable to move, as the horror continues. Loud. Ugly. Brutal.

He passes out.

He recovers. The violence has ended. The hard-faced

man is gone. He stumbles over to help Camille.

Stumbles into the bathroom looking for something to clean the blood away.

Sees the dead body of a woman in the bath.

He falls to his knees. Blood, pain and shock overtake him.

Then there is noise.

Rushing feet.

People.

He blacks out.

..

He is in a crowded car, being driven at speed. Camille is with him.

He passes out again.

..

It is night.

He is in a room. Clean. Tidy.

Safe.

Camille is sat at a table across the room. She has been cleaned up, and is talking to another woman.

A young man approaches, brings him a cup of coffee.

The young man tells him that Camille is fine. Her body will heal as the day resets. All other wounds will heal with time. He tells him that she has given them both of their addresses, and that come morning, each of them will be met, and proper introductions will be made.

The young man looks up at a clock on the wall.

..

He wakes.

Remembers.

The knock on the door comes even before the kettle has boiled. Scully closes the living room door, hiding the body of his mother from view, then answers the front door.

The young man is there. A car is waiting.

..

They are at the house. Coffee, tea and biscuits around a large farmhouse-style wooden kitchen table. A group of a dozen or so, friendly people, plus Scully and Camille.

Camille won't look at him, or acknowledge him. She sits away from him. Her physical wounds have disappeared, but her eyes are cold and dark.

An older man speaks, introducing the group to the visitors.

He tells them how the original group had reset that first time to a late-night dinner party, around that same table, which had rambled on into the early hours.

That was about four years ago.

Since then, they have learned a lot. Not about whatever had happened to them, and keeps happening, but about what happens in the world.

Like what happens when bad people get caught in the day, and realise that there are no repercussions when they do bad things.

Over time they have brought in new members to their group, and now they work together to protect themselves and other people as much as possible from the small number of mad, bad, or otherwise dangerous people intent on abusing their situation to cause pain, misery and worse.

Obviously, they aren't always successful, but they insist they will work hard to ensure that what happened 'yesterday' would never happen again.

An invitation to join them in their work is offered to the new guests.

Camille doesn't turn to look at Scully.

..

He wakes.

Remembers.

He doesn't smile.

He sits in the room with the body. In the dark. In silence. Peeks through the curtains, watching the world go by.

He drinks.

He cries.

He turns on the television to drown out the silence.

He drinks.

He tells his mother that this is all her fault. If she hadn't been such a fucking nagging bitch, he wouldn't have killed her, and probably the next day would have been tomorrow, rather than the same fucking today.

He drinks more, and grows more angry. Shouting at her. Screams. Accuses. Curses.

Until all he has left are tears, and he falls, sobbing, over the body. On the television, people are happy, blissfully unaware that tomorrow will never come.

He wakes.

He lies in bed, making ugly, miserable-faced snow angels on the sheets.

There's a knocking at his front door.

She is there.

She punches him in the mouth.

Her follow-up smile tells him she's flirting.

They fuck, hard and loud, television blaring, and the dead body silent in the middle of the room.

Afterwards, drunk and naked in his bedroom, she tells him that the group had bored her senseless. Too fucking goody-two-shoes, prim and proper, saving-the-world type boring pricks. She had wanted to smash each one in the face with a hammer by mid-morning.

He reminds her that Eric knows where she lives; knows that the place they burned was hers. He asks her what she will do if he shows up there. She tells him that her first act every morning now is to grab a knife from the kitchen. From now on she's going to be ready for trouble.

He tells her he's proud of her.

She tells him to fuck her again.

Today is a good day.

..

They are sitting naked in bed, playing video games.

She tells him that their situation is not all bad.

They never have to go to work.

He responds. They never have to pay any bills.

She's thankful that she never has to wash her clothes.

He's thankful that the body downstairs never rots.

32

They both think that's hilarious.

..

She wakes, stares up at the ceiling, eyes following the cracks, taking in the familiar mould stains.

She smiles.

She heads to the kitchen, taking a small, sharp knife from the drawer before returning to her bedroom to get dressed.

Her phone rings. She picks it up. Holds it to her ear.

It speaks.

Long time no see.

Her bowels turn to ice.

She vomits.

..

She paces in the grim, piss-stained alley.

She is terrified. She chain-smokes cigarettes lit with a lighter held by a hand which won't stop shaking.

Her jaw trembles. Her eyes are red.

It begins to rain.

He appears. She watches in fear as he approaches.

Her fingers drop the lighter. He takes the cigarette from her lips. Takes a heavy drag. Draws the glowing end close to her face for a moment, before flicking it aside.

His name is Malik.

Her eyes never leave his.

He dominates her. Moves closer. Crushes her body against the wall with his. He doesn't speak.

She doesn't speak.

A passing pedestrian sees them. Senses the mood. Lowers his gaze and walks on. He saw nothing.

He tells her it's been too long. He kisses her.

She turns her face away. He pulls it back. Kisses her hard.

She kisses him back.

Later, she has a fresh bruise on her face.

They're sitting in the park. Watching the world continue to go by.

Malik rolls a spliff. One hand is roughly bandaged. Dirty. Blood-soaked. Congealed.

He takes a heavy toke on the joint. Passes it to her.

She inhales.

Exhales. Smoke thick and heavy.

He tells her he has died again since last they spoke. He had pushed a small child into traffic, and laughed until the coalescing mob beat his body into a bloody mess.

She watches the ignorant. Feeding ducks. Jogging.

Laughing like the world hasn't stopped.

She imagines herself screaming, holding the duck-feeder's head under the water until his decrepit body ceases its thrashing. She finds herself unmoved. This makes her sad.

He's been speaking to her. She hasn't taken in a word. She takes another toke, passes it on.

She imagines herself looking down at the shocked dead face of the drowned duck-feeder. She imagines the screams of onlookers, horrified at death in daylight. She imagines her own face. Scrutinises it until she finally sees the birth of a tear in the corner of one of her cold, dead eyes.

She stands. Tells him not to come again. Turns and walks away without looking at him.

He watches her go. Calls out after her. Tells her he has something he needs to tell her. When she ignores him he flicks the joint away and follows. He takes his time.

..

Scully is sitting on his doorstep, waiting for her when she gets there. She runs to him. Holds him violently tight. He holds her back. He doesn't ask.

He leads her indoors.

He doesn't notice that she's been followed.

..

She tells him the man with the blood-soaked bandage is Malik. An abuser she had fled from long ago. Only not so long ago. Time means something different now.

One day, long after she'd found herself caught in the day, she'd literally bumped into him in the street. He had been in a distressed state, jabbering frantically, fearfully, about being trapped in a day which seemed to be caught on a loop.

One of his fingers was bloody. He'd told her the tip had been sliced off as he woke, and had disappeared. He was terrified, his face stained with tears, snot and mud.

She'd backed away, horrified by what she'd seen. He

had shouted after her. Pleaded. Begged for her help. When she turned her back on him, his pleas turned to threats. Ugly, vicious threats.

When he'd screamed that he would cut her from her throat to her cunt, she ran. Pedestrians averted their attention. Crossed the street. She ran blindly, chased by his vile, despicable curses.

She tells Scully about the phone call. The fraught meeting in the dirty alley. Fucking the man with the bloody bandage wrapped around his hand.

She starts to cry. Tells him she doesn't know why she did it.

Scully knows she's hiding. She sees. Tells him it's a lie. She knows why.

She tells him she fucked Malik because he scares her. Always has. For her, fear is a trigger. A fuck trigger. She pulls Scully's hands to her throat, tells him she wants him to fuck her like that. She's still crying. Begging him to do it.

He fucks her because she needs him to.

38

When it's over, he holds her while she cries.

..

Later, while she sleeps, he smokes, watches the world go by from his bedroom window. The street is as the street always is.

Except, it isn't.

There in the street, smoking, staring right back at him. A man, one hand wrapped in a blood-soaked bandage.

Smiling.

He checks that she is asleep, then walks out to meet Malik.

He stops, just a few feet away. Their eyes lock.

Scully tells the bandaged man he won't let him hurt Camille.

Malik tells him that's not why he's here.

Then why?

Malik slowly unwraps the bloody rag from his hand, exposing the fresh wounds.

Only the thumb and index finger are unscathed.

The other fingers are most definitely scathed.

Scully sees the man's bloody stump, and asks again. Why?

Malik begins to re-wrap the rag around his hand, offering, as he does so, his own story.

In short, that the first day he woke into the Day, he woke screaming in pain. A sliver of flesh from his little finger had been sliced clean off, and had disappeared. The same thing had happened the next morning, and the next, and every inevitable pain-filled morning since then.

That was about two years ago.

He holds up his bloody stump.

This was what had been sliced off this morning.

They both stare at the hand.

This is different.

..

She wakes.

She takes two knives today.

She leaves without her phone, on purpose.

She heads to Scully's house. Knocks rapidly on his door. He's there. She holds him tight.

This is the only place where she feels safe.

He leads her into the kitchen.

Where the man with the bloody, rag-wrapped stump is sitting, drinking a cup of tea.

She freezes. Begins to retch.

Scully comforts her. Tells her Malik isn't here to hurt, but to help.

She steps forward, spits into Malik's face, then turns and walks out of the kitchen.

Scully follows, gently takes her arm, leads her into the front room. Holds her, whispering comfort in the dark, curtained room where his mother lies, open-eyed and eternal.

The two of them step back into the kitchen. Malik has finished wiping the spittle spray from his face.

She sits.

They all sit, waiting.

Camille feels naked. Exposed. The silence in the room is somehow humiliating.

Scully breaks the edge. Says to Malik.

Tell her.

Malik tells her.

Tells her how the Day is no longer just the Day. That something is changing. Tells her that over the past

42

thirty-something days, each morning has left him with less flesh, fewer digits on his hand. The pain is the same searing horror when each morning comes, but now there is a deep, rumbling dread as he realises he is being eaten away, and can do nothing to stop the Day from devouring him.

Camille says nothing. All three ponder in silence what this means to them. To their world. To their lives in the Day.

The only sound inside the house is that of a clock, ticking ironically, in the room where a corpse lies discarded on the carpet.

..

They sit, mid-morning, in a drab cafe which stinks of grease and cigarettes. The tables are sticky with an assortment of filth. The tea is weak, and the waitress seems to ooze contempt.

They sit surrounded by misery, compounding their mood. They are afraid. The sight of Malik's bandaged hand, bloodstains being slowly added to by tabletop pollutants, fills their guts with choking, turbulent dread.

The Day is changing. More than that. It is...

It is attacking them. Now, they are not merely prisoners. Now they are prey. With each waking scream, Malik is being eaten alive, though none of them knows by what.

The others are filled to the dry core of their bones with the fear that their next waking moment will be filled with those same screams. The same removal of flesh and bone. Or worse. Each imagines so much more worse.

Scully looks around. Watches the grim faces of their fellow customers in that miserable place. Their faces are each stained with a life which has disappointed, but none show the marks of torture at the hands of recurring temporal evil.

Why us? He asks. Why not everybody?

Slowly, they begin to see what is before them in a way they have not seen before. They imagine that this creature which has been devouring them is not a single entity, but is perhaps a group. A pack. A swarm.

So, again. Why us? Why not all of us? Why now?

What? How? Why? Their ignorance of their attacker and their fate poisons mind and soul, and they are no closer to answers than before they asked.

..

The evening is threatening to turn into night, and Malik's terror at the fast-approaching morning screams loud across the tension-thick air between them.

They are sat at a bus stop, watching the world unfurl its chaos, seeking answers within the mêlée. Electric light illuminates the terrifying darkness of night, silhouetting the untouched, unconcerned crowd which passes on by, but no answers come.

They bid Malik goodnight, leaving him at the stop. Neither can bear to wait as fear overtakes him at the rapid approach of morning.

..

Scully wakes with a scream in his throat. He grabs each hand with the other, rapidly checking that his fingers are still there. Eight, nine, ten. Relief almost chokes him to tears.

He had been dreaming. He isn't sure that he has dreamt before. Not since the Day began. He is terrified.

He only recollects a few sparse, suggested fragments of dream, but those few memories spike his guts with fear. Images of waking to find his fingers gone, only bloody stumps left, pulsating in agony. He forces down his tears, locking them inside with his screams, and dresses quickly. He heads downstairs and out of the house without pausing his step to check the room for the body of his dead mother.

He races to Camille, meeting her on an unconcerned street halfway between his house and hers, and together they walk - briskly, hand-in-sweaty-hand - to Malik's address.

They stand outside his door, on the fifth floor of a degraded block of flats, the stink of rotten concrete overpowering the harsh stench of urine. They stand there, each willing themselves to raise a hand to knock, each too frightened to have that knock go unanswered.

They listen. The entire floor seems deserted. There is no sound. No signs of life coming from beyond the door, from Malik's flat. Camille and Scully stand transfixed before the door, the thunder of their own heartbeats pounding in their ears. They feel dizzy.

This is what real terror feels like. Each thinks it, though neither can speak the words.

When he can take the terror no more, Scully raises one clenched fist, and raps on the scruffy green door. His lips move slightly, betraying the mantra uttered silently within himself, to himself, to Malik, to the Day and to any god which would deign to listen to somebody like him : please let there be an answer - any answer, any suggestion that the darkest of fears has not manifested as petrifying reality.

There is no answer. Just the sound of the knock echoing over and over again inside them, adding to the overwhelming noise of their fast-beating hearts.

Of course, the door is locked. Who would leave their

door open in a place like this? Even though the floor seems deserted. Not a person in sight or the sound of one moving about. What if the same madness lives behind each of these doors? What horrors could the Day have wrought?

Scully braces himself, then races at the door. It is an old door, and cheap. It bursts open on the first attempt, offering them entry, but cutting deep into Scully's flesh with ugly, jagged splinters. Blood flows, and Scully screams curses at his own life.

After the curses fade, leaving only throbbing pain, and blood, Scully and Camille stand in the hallway, and listen. There is still no sound. No response to their violent, noisy, forced entry. Either Malik had left his flat early - even now he could be knocking at one or another of their doors, wondering where they are - or...

Or.

The two trespassers link their fingers tightly, and move along the hallway towards the door at the end of the passage - ajar slightly, letting them know that this is Malik's bedroom.

They stop just outside the room. Hands clench tighter, painfully so.

After the longest, breathless, pause, Scully reaches up with one free hand, and gently pushes the door open.

They stand at the entrance to the room, motionless but for their perfidious eyes, which take in the scene of ugly violence before them, force-feeding them the details of the desperate suffering and agonies to which only they and the room bear witness.

Only a little over half of Malik remains on the blood-soaked bed. It is as though a circle had been drawn around him, a dreadful arc cutting through his chest, removing one arm and a shoulder completely, and slicing across his abdomen. At some point, that which was Malik which had been outside of the circle had ceased to be, and what remained was free to bleed out profusely, slopping fluids and organs and unidentifiable mess across the dirty never-white sheets in a grim tableau of carnage. Malik's face is frozen in a grimace of one final, shocked scream.

The onlookers perform as one a synchronised performance of projectile vomiting, the contents of their stomachs joining the blood and the flesh, mingling. They fall to their knees, retching uncontrollably. With the vomit comes a horrified sobbing, and both add tears to the mélange of flesh and fluids soaking into the sheets.

..

The same mid-morning, another grim and greasy cafe filled with the ill and the desperate and the unfortunate. Neither can bear to be where people laugh and joke and live their lives oblivious to the Day. Neither can stomach the sights and sounds of the joys of life, not when their eyes, memories and souls are stained with the sight of Malik's final Day.

They sit. Facing each other, but neither looking at the other. Each mind is locked back in that room. Each knows that the next time they wake, they may suffer the same fate, and that there is no way they can run. Not from Time. Not from the endlessly-approaching morning.

..

Scully wakes, and remembers. He curls into a ball, and

begins to cry.

Camille wakes, and remembers. She lies motionless. Her eyes, looking up at the patches of mould on her ceiling, fill with tears, and overflow.

..

Scully wakes. He has a routine now. He checks his room for the slightest difference. Checks his body for cuts or wounds. Any sign that all is not as it has been for so long.

He dresses. Makes his way downstairs. Closes the door to the room where his mother lies in eternal silence. Makes himself a coffee, seats himself at the kitchen table, and waits.

He has no idea what he's waiting for, or even if he'll recognise it if it arrives, but at least if he stays here, he might fool himself into thinking that he can be safe. That the Day will not turn on him as it had done to Malik.

He has not seen Camille since the morning they discovered Malik's tortured corpse. She, in turn, has not turned up at his door. His life is silent now, but for the ticking of the clock in the other room, and the endless screaming inside his head.

When his coffee is cold, he pours it out, and makes himself a fresh cup. He sits at the kitchen table, cradling the cup. When that cup is cold, he repeats the process. When evening comes, he washes the cup, and heads to bed. He does not sleep, for the longest time, until it's almost time, then

he wakes. He has a routine now. He checks his room for the slightest difference. Checks his body for cuts or wounds. Any sign that all is not as it has been for so long.

He dresses. Makes his way downstairs.   Closes the door to the room where his mother lies in eternal silence. Makes himself a coffee, seats himself at the kitchen table, and waits.

When his coffee is cold, he pours it out, and makes himself a fresh cup. He sits at the kitchen table, cradling the cup. When that cup is cold, he repeats the process. When evening comes, he washes the cup, and heads to bed. He does not sleep, for the longest time, until it's almost time, then

he wakes. He has a routine now. He checks his room for the slightest difference. Checks his body for cuts or wounds. Any sign that all is not as it has been for so long.

He dresses. Makes his way downstairs. Closes the door to the room where his mother lies in eternal silence. Makes himself a coffee, seats himself at the kitchen table, and waits.

He wonders to himself. How long has it been? How many days have passed since the first Day? Since his first Day?

How many mornings has he woken with the just-dead body of his mother lying in the room below? He realises that he can barely remember what she had looked like when she was alive. For too many days, all he has seen of her has been the still, silent body, frozen mid-nag. One vivid bruise around the patch of broken skin on the side of her head where he'd hit her with the hammer.

He no longer feels the rage he once did. No longer

curses her for trapping him in the Day. For driving him to murder, and for all which followed. He has found some kind of peace, though not one most people would recognise. It's the kind of peace he supposes he would feel if he were to suddenly encounter a speeding train heading towards him, mere feet away. An acceptance of a horrific, painful end which cannot be avoided.

Once again, he toys with the notion that he is, perhaps, dead. That this is the Eternity promised for those such as him.

So deep in thought is he, that he barely registers the knocking at first. It takes him a while until he realises that someone is at his front door.

A young man is there. Clean. Composed. Familiar.

The young man tells Scully that his name is Aaron. Scully remembers, then. The farmhouse table. The group. What did Camille call them? A bunch of goody-two-shoes, saving-the-world type boring pricks? He laughs, but invites Aaron in anyway.

The young man tells Scully that he's here to take him to the house. He tells him that everybody will be there.

Scully tells the young man to fuck off, and for a brief moment, his rage returns.

Aaron says that they know about Malik. Tells him that all of those trapped by the Day share the same grief. The same need to mourn both Malik and themselves. The same dread that they will share the same fate.

Scully looks closer, sees the screaming fear behind the young man's eyes, and relents.

..

The room is full. There are perhaps thirty or so people there, talking in a number of groups. Scully recognises some of the faces from when he was here last.

With a spasm of shock, he recognises the man that he and Camille had stabbed to death on a street so long ago. It is the same man, but this time his face is not distorted with madness and rage. He seems calm, almost happy.

Then he sees her.

From across the room, she sees him. She offers him a

small, but warm, smile, then makes her way through the bodies towards him, silently offering her hand to his. Their fingers link once more. She tells him she has missed him. He tells her he has missed her too. He realises just how much he has missed her as he feels the warmth of her arm pressed against his.

There is a faint susurration from among the crowd, and Scully and Camille look up to see an older man enter the room. They both recognise him from their previous visit. He introduces himself, to those who may not yet know him, as Caspian. He speaks softly, but receives absolute attention from the listeners in the room.

Caspian tells those gathered of the story of the group, from the first night a small number of them were reborn into the Day around a familiar table, through confusion and uncertainty and tragedy, to the organised body of men and women who now work tirelessly to help and protect those suffering from their temporal incarceration.

He speaks of finding those enduring violence and brutal despair - the victims, in his eyes, being those who are driven to impose it as well as those receiving it. He speaks of helping those dragged into insanity by the Day, and those lost to terror and confusion.

Soon, others take their turn to speak, offering their stories. Men and women tell their stories of their own, particular Day. Some have been trapped for weeks, others for months.

Then a young, well-presented man begins to speak. Scully is struck with a sense of familiarity, yet cannot place the man. Only as his story develops does Scully realise that this is the same rambling madman he watched in secret, babbling his own angry narration of his Day from the squalor of his wasteland home.

The young man's name is Stephan. He speaks with the same gentle tones as Caspian, but with more care taken to control his speech, as though he is afraid he might slip once more into angry, hostile rambling if he falters.

He tells the hushed room of his Day. How he woke on wasteland where he had been sleeping rough for some time, only vaguely aware that something had gone wrong with the world. How he thought he had become mad, that his life and its wretchedness had tipped him over the edge into a broken state. But his Day continued, and persisted. He tells them he long ago lost count of the number of times he has killed himself, ending his life each day only to find it there again come morning. He tells of being found by members of the group, and gradually brought to a place of ease - how now he wakes on the same patch of wasteland, but with the knowledge that friends are nearby, and that with that knowledge comes some kind of hope.

In his best estimation, he tells them, he has been held in the Day for around forty-two years.

The collected guests in the room take this information in in silence.

After a while, Scully breaks the silence.

What about Malik?

All eyes turn to Scully.

What about Malik? he repeats. This mutual appreciation society is all fine and dandy, but what about the fact that this shit isn't just an inconvenience? What about the fact that we had to see a guy's insides poured out across his bed because he'd been sawn in half by this fucking thing?

Do any of you actually know what the fuck is going on? Do any of you have a clue why it's happening? Why us? How many of us are there? How many of us are being cut into pieces by whatever this fucking thing is?

Scully is suddenly aware of the looks on the faces of the crowd, and realises that not only is he shouting, but he's crying, and Camille is standing with him, gripping his hand tightly, shedding her own tears.

That's the moment when his knees buckle, sobs erupt from him, and he falls to the floor, crying like a child in pain : I killed my mum.

..

They don't react the way he would have expected them to. Once his tears have dried, leaving only shame and embarrassment, he is met not with revulsion, but empathy. They understand. Or, at least they think they do. Perhaps many have been led to murder and other horrors through the onslaught of the Day, but none of them had struck a fatal blow prior to the start of their new state of being. He is different. He knows it.

But he hides it. Lets them comfort him. Allows them to offer warm words of encouragement, but feeling already the cold stab of hatred beginning to grow in his belly. Knows already that the more they seek to welcome him into their familial embrace, the more he will despise them for it, and the more he will despise himself for doing so.

Caspian takes the floor once more.

He offers to the assembled body the opportunity to mourn the passing of one of their own. A fellow prisoner of the unending Day. They bow their heads for a moment, and the room is silent.

..

Later, Scully and Camille sit together, hand-in-hand on a park bench, watching people pass by. Scully tells her that he no longer feels that he is real. That anything is real. That the world seems to be nothing more than ink painted on a bubble, and he's just waiting for it to pop.

She says nothing, but grips his hand a little more

tightly. He feels a little better, but still can't hold back the tears.

..

Scully wakes. He has a routine now. He checks his room for the slightest difference. Checks his body for cuts or wounds. Any sign that all is not as it has been for so long.

Something is different.

He looks carefully around at his room, squinting through the early morning light, seeing that everything is in its place. All is where it should be. He checks his body again for cuts, for any sign of something different. Nothing. He has no wounds, no bruises.

But, all the same...

something is different.

When he realises what it is, his body locks in fear. He is paralysed, his thoughts racing.

The light is different.

The light is different.

The light is different.

Every morning the light is the same. He wakes at the same moment. The light is the same.

The light is different.

This is a different time.

His breathing is rapid. Harsh. He feels as though he is about to black out. Hope, violently excited hope, is killing him. He concentrates, forces his breaths to slow their pace. Forces himself towards a state of pseudo-calm.

He sits up, and carefully eases himself out of bed, heads towards the stairs, and descends. The difference in light is subtle, but it's there. He edges towards the room, peers around the side of the door.

Sees her lifeless body lying there as it had forever.

But, it could still be tomorrow. He hasn't bothered moving her body for the longest time. He walks to the window. Watches the street.

For the briefest of moments, it is new. Different. Unseen before.

Then the Day begins to unfold as always, and shattered, diseased Hope stabs harshly into his gut, causing him intense physical pain.

As his day begins again, Scully screams.

..

Later, while sitting at his kitchen table, cradling a cold cup of coffee, he is surprised by a gentle, tentative knock on his door.

When he sees her face, he begins to cry.

..

He is more composed now. His tears locked away inside himself, where they should be. On his face he wears a smile as he sits at the table with Camille. She reaches out and holds his hand, pulls it to her lips and kisses it. She seems happy, despite everything. He wonders how she does it. She smiles. He smiles back.

..

Crouched conspiratorially across a table at another half-empty cafe, he tells her of his morning. He tells her how the light was different. That new moments had presented themselves. That this was something new. She is worried, desperately so. She grips his hand tightly. He smiles at her concern for him. He tells her that, somehow, for the first time in so long, he has a feeling that this can end well. That there may be other ways for this to end than being...

...it doesn't have to end as it had for Malik.

He smiles again, and she grips his hand tighter still, her nails hard against his skin. He feels the rush in his body once more. She sees it, and feels it too. He tells her he wants to fuck her right there. They race at each other in a manic frenzy of violent, needful lust, ripping at each other's clothes, tearing. They fuck hard there on the filthy floor, while the other diners look away, afraid.

..

Later, lying naked in his bed, he tells her of the darkness of his days without her. He tells her he wants her to stay. Wants her to keep staying. Wants to know if their Days can merge into one. That way, they could always be together, no matter what the Day threw at them, they could face it together. She loves him for asking, and tells him so. She kisses him. He kisses her.

He wakes, feeling her kiss on his lips. But it is an illusion. She's not there. He's alone.

But the light is different.

Not just different to his usual Day, but different to the Day which had just passed.

Scully laughs out loud.

..

They spend that day together. They talk. They laugh. They fuck like teenagers. There is something new in the air. Something good. He tells her he loves her. She squeals with laughter, and kisses him over and over.

..

He wakes. Dresses quickly, and rushes out into the street. It is raining. He has never woken while it was still raining before. He laughs as he dances in the miraculous downpour.

A cyclist, pedalling through the semi-darkness of the early morning, watches as Scully dances. The cyclist smiles, and passes on by.

After a while, Scully heads back into the house. He is drenched, but ecstatic. He races into the living room, to where his mother lies lifeless. He tells her, excitedly. Mum, It's going to be okay. Something is happening. Be happy for me. He kisses her cold, clammy face. Tells her he forgives her for everything. Then he dances away, into the kitchen, smiling.

That morning, he reaches her place soon after she wakes, surprising her. She makes them breakfast. They sit together and eat, as if everything was normal. As if this was not *the* Day, but just *a* day. They walk out together, breathing in the sweet morning air. He says hello to strangers they pass in the street. She holds his hand. They smile so much it hurts.

They buy food. Have lunch as a picnic in the park, as

much a part of the crowd as any of the other couples enjoying the sunshine on the grass. Soft kisses and sunshine and blue skies.

A perfect day.

Scully smiles as he lays back on the grass, feeling her warm body nestled against his. His fingers stroke hers, making her giggle.

He wakes.

He jumps up quickly, suddenly alert. His heart is racing. Why is the morning here already? What happened to the rest of his Day? His perfect day?

He dresses in a rush, runs out into the deserted street. This is wrong. This is nowhere near morning. This is pre-dawn night. With dread clawing at his racing heart, he runs through the streets.

He reaches her door, and begins to hammer hard on it, screaming, begging for her to let him in. She doesn't answer. A nagging, undefined terror grips him. Why isn't she answering? He slams his fist hard against her door. A neighbour, woken from sleep, shouts from their window for him to be quiet. He tells them harshly to fuck off, and continues his assault on the door. When there is still no answer, he punches a hole in the glass pane to the side of the door, slicing open his hand, and reaches in to open the door. His hand slips on the catch, sticky now with his blood, but he perseveres, and the door swings open. He rushes inside, calling out her name.

Then a light is switched on, and he sees her. She stands there in the hallway, dripping wet bathwater. Half-dressed, holding a knife, shaking in fear. He moves towards her, and she raises the blade.

Wide-eyed, she screams at him.

Who the fuck are you?

He feels as though he has been slapped hard in the face. He tries to speak, but nothing comes out. He stands in her living room, silently dripping blood onto her carpet.

She repeats, in a frightened snarl.

Who the fuck are you?

Tears well up in his eyes. He wipes them away with his hand, and smears blood across his face.

Without saying a word, he turns and runs. He doesn't look back. He runs through the night-time streets, his lungs tearing as he screams as he runs as he screams.

In a street he's never been to before, he stops. He falls to his knees, barely feeling the searing pain as his knees hit the cold stone pavement, and his body shakes with the deep, wailing sobs ripping through him.

..

When morning comes, he is sitting at his kitchen table, cradling a cup of coffee, one hand roughly bandaged. His mind is a torrent of confusion. He is lost. Absolutely lost.

There is a frantic knocking at his door. He ignores it. It continues. After a while he gets up, trudges to the door with menace in his heart. He opens the door.

She rushes in, gripping him in a tight hug, her words unintelligible through her tears. He stands with her in the doorway, confused and tearful.

They sit together at the table, facing one another with hands linked and trembling. She tells him she had thought him gone forever. She tells him of that moment the previous afternoon when, while lying together in the most perfect day, when he had simply ceased to be. One moment he was warm beside her, the next she was alone. She had searched the park, raced to his house and battered on his door, but he was nowhere. She tells him how she returned to the same spot in the park, and lay there as night approached, waiting for him. How he never came, and then there was morning, and the Day.

When she has finished, he tells her of his new Day. He tells her how he ran to be with her, only to find a terrified stranger.

She sees the pain in his eyes as he tells her how she had not recognised him. She tells him she remembers something, perhaps from a dream, before the Day. A shadow of a memory from a night so long ago.

She sees the pain on his face as he tells her of his fear that there might come a time when their Days no longer overlap. That each morning he will wake and she will not know him. And what of her? Will she wake in her Day to find that he no longer exists? Or will she be faced with what he will become by the time - if ever - he escapes his own Day?

They sit in silence, contemplating dark futures.

As afternoon approaches, they make their plans. She tells him all she can remember of the time before her Day. She tells him how he might approach her to convince her he is not a stranger. He tells her he loves her. They embrace with ferocity, their bodies crushed together in defiance of their fate. In defiance of the Day.

He wakes.

He races once more through the night to her door. Calls through her letterbox, using a name she hasn't used since she was a girl.

This time she comes to the door. She doesn't open it. It is night, and she is afraid. Curious, but afraid.

He tells her things he could not know. He tells her that she need not be afraid. For the longest time there is silence from behind the door. He sees her still standing there through the mottled glass which before had sliced his hand open.

She opens the door, but not fully. She is still afraid, but her curious eyes ponder him through the crack she has opened between them. Then she opens it fully, and wordlessly invites him in.

He sees she is holding the knife. He smiles. He likes that she is prepared to defend herself.

They stand there in the room, facing one another, barely three feet apart. She is assessing him. He is loving the sight of her in this, the day before her Day.

She asks him questions. He answers as best he can. She sees honesty in his eyes.

He tells her of the day. Of the two of them. Of the fucking. Of the pain and blood and horror. Of love.

She believes him. She's not sure why, but she does. She sets the blade down, and moves closer to him, her eyes never leaving his. He tells her they don't have long. Soon she will vanish from that Day, and wake at the beginning of another, while he will return home, and wait for her there come morning.

He feels her warm embrace once more.

..

As daylight returns, he is assembling breakfast. On his way back home he had stopped, bought croissants and good coffee. He whistles as he sets the table for them both. He sets the door on the latch for her. He sits and waits, his new smile never once leaving his face.

She doesn't knock, but rushes through the door, into the kitchen and into his arms, laughing and crying and squeezing him as tightly as she can, and he holds her, burying his face in her neck. They kiss, kiss again, in a ferocious rush. She drags him upstairs to his bed, and they laugh while they fuck, naked and happy, and the coffee goes cold, and the croissants sit uneaten on the kitchen table.

Life is good.

Later, she lies naked on top of him, the two of them sharing a cigarette. She tells him how she woke with a memory of the night before her Day began. She tells him that it seems as though the memory has always been there. She is excited. Playful. Young again. She laughs, blows smoke in his face. She wriggles atop him. He gets hard again.

Later still, they walk in the sunshine, hand in hand. She knows he has to go, and he knows that he will have to work again to make himself known to her as a stranger, but each knows that when the other goes, they will race through the streets to be together again.

The sunlight warms the air, and in it he can smell her perfume.

He wakes. The room is in darkness. He smiles the broadest of smiles.

He estimates that it has been about ten days since he began to wake earlier. Ten days since he began to romance Camille on both sides of her Day. He told her at one point that he felt guilty at times, as if he were sleeping with two women. She told him that turned her on. She held him down and made him fuck her while he told her what he was going to do to her on the other side of her Day.

..

He is standing in a 24-hour supermarket - brightly-lit, though almost deserted apart from a bored cashier and a couple of kids avoiding the cctv to steal chocolate bars and crisps.

He buys her flowers. He hopes it's not too much. He's gotten used to the late-night romancing of the stranger he knows so well, but every time is the first time for her. Every time he needs to convince her, to be honest and to show her who he is, but he is a man in love, and he has a hard time hiding it.

The bored cashier takes his money, and Scully heads to the door. As it opens for him, a man walks in, eyes downcast to the floor, passing Scully without looking up. Scully almost stumbles as shock freezes his limbs, but in a moment he recovers, and he strides quickly away from the supermarket. All the time, his mind is screaming in horror.

It is the same man. The one they had stabbed so long ago. The one so full of madness and rage, with the Munchian scream. The one so different when the group met around the farmhouse table. Only now...

Now that man is broken. There is pain in his eyes, and at the end of one arm there is a bloody, bandaged stump. The sight of it brings back memories of Malik, and the horrors they had seen that morning, staring at his mutilated body painted across the sheets like an abominable canvas.

Scully had forgotten the fear. He had forgotten the wrenching in the gut which came from realising that their situation was not without the possibility of ugly, vicious suffering. That this thing could literally eat them alive.

Now he remembers.

He sits at the side of the road, crouched on the pavement, pulling hard on a cigarette. He exhales, smoke filling the air around him. He tries to stop himself from shaking, but only ends up crying softly to himself as the cigarette butt drops into the gutter.

When he is empty of tears, he brushes the wetness from his face. He composes himself, for her sake, picks up the flowers he has bought, and walks through the lamplit streets to a place where love and smiles banish the demons of blood and pain and death.

..

He wakes. For the first time since his Day began, he notices the ringing of church bells in the distance. He counts them. It is three o'clock in the morning.

He turns over, half-expecting her to be beside him, warm and naked, where she had been just moments ago. But, of course, she isn't there. The bed is cold, as it always is come morning.

He is tired. He feels as though he hasn't slept in months. Each morning he wakes, rushes to make himself known to Camille, spends the remainder of the dark hours with her until just before she vanishes, then heads home, where he prepares himself for the rest of the day with her in her Day, until he disappears from her life, and the cycle restarts.

Once, he had weakly suggested that perhaps he might stay. That perhaps he could be there when the day before her Day ended, and when her Day began. That they could lie there as though it was the most natural thing in the world. But both were scared to try. Neither knew how the change in the Day manifested itself, or what could happen to them in the moment when before-the-Day became the Day. Malik's changing Day, and the consequences of it, had left them with a deep, gut-gnawing dread of what could happen if something were to go wrong. If they were to step out of line. If they were to challenge the gods of the Day. They never mentioned it again.

..

He wakes. He listens.

He smiles when he hears the bells. He had hoped it would be so. Two bells. Two o'clock.

He races through the streets, his breathing harsh and painful. Every moment counts. He finds it ironic that he lives an endless life in an immortal Day, yet finds himself stealing all the time he can from every single morning, just to be with her.

He stops abruptly, doubling over in pain, struggling to catch his breath. He smiles, realising that he's not as fit as he once was, despite the fact that he never actually gets any older.

Once his breathing has returned to normal, and the fire

in his lungs has subsided to a fierce, dull ache, he begins slowly to jog towards Camille's place, to woo her once more. He smiles again to himself as he catches himself hoping she doesn't fall for him too quickly. He tells himself he can barely breathe, let alone satisfy Camille's frantic sexual appetite.

He ponders on her appetite, and begins to jog a little more quickly.

..

Later, having spent a few precious hours rekindling their love affair once again, and revelling in its newness, he is back at home, sat at the table in his kitchen, waiting for her. His spirits are high, the sun is shining and the smell of fresh coffee permeates the room.

He waits.

She is late. There is no welcoming rush through his door, no tight embrace.

The ticking of the clock in the other room suddenly sounds ominous.

He tells himself it's okay. There's a good reason for her being late. But he knows he cannot mask the fear clutching at his insides.

He runs to her.

He doesn't want her to feel his fear, and so when he reaches her door, he knocks with as much nonchalance as he can muster. But he is afraid.

She answers, and he almost cries with relief. He reaches out to her

and sees the towel wrapped around her shoulder.

Blood staining the pea-green fabric.

They stand there for the longest time, knowing eyes locked together, filling with tears.

Later, he bathes her, gently cleaning her wound, comforting her with warm water and bubbles as if they could soothe away the fear she feels.

They spend the first part of the afternoon in bed. He holds her. She cries, softly.

..

He wakes

He is terrified. His heart is racing. He finds it hard to breathe.

He screams his rage and impotence to the empty room and an uncaring Day, knowing that Camille would have had to spend almost half her Day alone, facing the fear of what was happening without him there to comfort her.

He knows he has to swallow his pain, his grief, his powerlessness and his blood-freezing fear for the Camille in her Day, because there is another Camille who needs him. A Camille who as yet knows nothing of the Day.

He dresses, and races through the night-time streets.

..

Later that morning, he sits with Camille as she lays in the bath. He gently sponges her wound, the flesh raw now from her shoulder to her wrist.

They spend the morning in silent contemplation of the slow-approaching horror. Each fights against the vision of Malik's end which seeks to overpower their senses.

They turn on the TV, and turn it up loud to drown out their own internal screams.

..

He wakes.

He wants to cry. For himself. For Camille. For them all, on either side of the Day. But he's too tired for the tears to come.

He's more tired than he's ever been. He stumbles from his bedroom to the top of the stairs.

He trips.

He falls head-first down the stairs. Feels a cheekbone crack. Feels blood pour into his eye. More stairs. Finger bones shatter. He screams.

He lands at the bottom of the stairs. His head spinning

from the pain. Every movement brings more agony. Still, he forces himself up until he is kneeling in the hallway, leaning against the wall for support. He knows he needs to run, to be with her, though he can barely see.

He cries out curses as he pulls his broken body to a standing position. Still relying on the wall to hold him up. He rests for a short while. Prepares himself for the onslaught of pain he knows he's about to endure.

Slowly, he makes his way along the corridor, inch by inch, to the front door. He fumbles at the catch with his unbroken fingers.

The door pops open. He steels himself for the run.

Then he hears it.

A faint sound.

Coming from the room.

He listens. Maybe he had imagined a sound. There's nothing there but silence.

Then he hears it again. Soft. Barely-there.

Slowly, he edges towards the doorway to the room. The pain coursing through him brings with it a tremendous nausea. He breathes hard to fight off the urge to vomit.

Then he leans close, and looks into the room.

It takes a while for his eyes to focus in the darkness. He listens hard, trying to block out the sound of his own heartbeat thundering in his head.

He listens.

He hears.

A low, soft sound, like gentle breathing.

In a flash of clarity, Scully realises that he's listening to his mother's final breaths. She is not yet dead.

His knees give way, and he tips forward. He puts out a hand to catch himself, and broken fingers break his fall. He screams, and vomits onto the carpet.

He screams. At her. At the world. At his life. Why the fuck won't you just die?

He cries in pain and helplessness. He feels as though he is broken beyond repair. Still, he forces himself up once more, turns his back on his dying mother, and stumbles out into the street.

..

He bathes her once more, cleaning her wounds while she cries in pain. He suggests they visit a hospital, but she tells him. No. She wants nobody but him. He senses that she is becoming delirious. Her wounds - her arm, one hand and part of a foot mangled and raw - are severe.

He lies with her as she shakes, and cries.

..

They spend their days in the park. When she can no longer walk, he steals her a wheelchair. They sit beside the duck pond, and she watches as he feeds the birds.

..

He wakes. In the early hours of the morning of his Day he calls on his other Camille. She sees how much he loves her, though she never understands how much, or why. He cannot bring himself to tell her what lies on the other side of morning. She knows he is hiding something terrible from her, but she sees the love in his eyes, merged with the pain, and she lets his secrets pass on by.

..

Camille is gone.

He sits on the floor beside her bed. He has her blood on him. On his hands, his clothes, his face. For so long he had lain close to her. To what was left of her. Feeling her warm flesh cool. Blood staining the sheets, dripping quietly to the floor.

He knows that she will no longer wake. That each new Day will merely leave less of her behind.

She still lives, as a stranger in the pre-Day night, but he cannot bear to be with her. Knowing that the Day will devour her mere hours after they meet. He cannot woo her. Cannot romance her. Cannot love her with the memory of her loss cutting him so deeply.

He sits on the floor beside her bed. He has no tears left inside. Nothing, but hollowness and loss.

He is empty. He is alone. He is a dead man forced to live through an everlasting Day.

..

He sits in his kitchen. He sits at the table, cradling an empty cup.

He doesn't drink. He doesn't eat.

He will stay here, for as long as it takes. Years. Centuries. Aeons. He knows that at some point, this must end. This one, infinite Day must end. The eddies and whorls of Time will collapse, leaving those who suffer now free from their grasp. There will be a Tomorrow. A day beyond the Day, as there were days before the Day. And then, when it is over, there will be Camille. And they will put the horrors of the Day behind them. And the sun will shine, or not shine. The future will be unknown, but they will be together, and they will lie naked together once more, and they will fuck and they will kiss and they will hold hands and laugh out loud at the strangeness of other days.

He sits in his kitchen. He sits at the table, cradling an empty cup.

Mondays

Mondays